For Paul Sidebotham

My dad,

Here is one of your stories finally in print.

You are gone you are not forgotten.

June 2020

This edition has been published by Gemma Moran

First published in 2020

Text copyright © Gemma Moran

Illustrations copyright © sarah Mellor

The Moral rights of Gemma Moran & Sarah Mellor have been asserted

The Race

Written by: Paul Sidebotham   Illustrated by: Sarah Mellor

Edited and Published by: Gemma Moran

In support of the
British Heart Foundation

A percentage of the sale of this book goes to the British Heart Foundation

Thumpitty was a lively rabbit, who thought there was nothing better than romping round the fields and running races with his friends to see who was the fastest.

Running alongside of the field where he lived was a rough bumpy road and the farmer who owned the field would drive his big car up and down this road on his way to and from the market during the day, and to and from the village at night.

All the mother rabbits were worried that their children might be hurt by the noisy, banging car and warned the young rabbits that they must never go through the tall hedge, which separated the field from the road.

Thumpitty had always run farther and faster than any of his fellows and was constantly boasting that he could run faster than the farmer's car.

When it appeared over the hill he would begin running; the car

bumping

and

thumping

along the road, and Thumpitty racing along on the other side of the hedge, to the corner of the field which marked the end of the race.

Sadly, just before the road dipped down, and even though Thumpitty's friends stretched on their hind legs, they could never see who reached the corner first.

Thumpitty felt sure that he always beat the car, but his pals would tease him because he ran and ran without knowing if he won.

The car would suddenly disappear from sight, into the dip, and for the last part of the race all they would be able to see was Thumpitty's little white tail bobbing brightly against the dark green grass.

One night Thumpitty lay in his warm
burrow, unable to sleep.

He kept remembering how his friends had teased him and decided to settle things once and for all.

So, forgetting all his mother's warnings, he slipped out of the burrow into the cold dark night and hopped slowly to the corner of the field.

He stopped when he came to the hedge, as he sat on the cold damp grass he thought longingly of his warm bed back in the burrow.

But he was a determined rabbit, so he squirmed his way through the hedge and onto the road.
He settled himself below the brow of the hill to wait, as he wasn't sure when the car would come.

At first ....

everything
seemed quiet,

when he pricked up
his ears, he could hear
all the strange nighttime noises
and was a little frightened.

Suddenly,

he heard a low rumbling sound coming from far away, so he pricked up his ears again to see if he could hear more clearly.

The sound grew louder, changing as it grew from a rumbling to a soft

"roar"

Thumpitty turned his head
to look at the top of
the hill, but could
see nothing except
the blackness
of the night sky.

The sound was
everywhere now
and louder still.

Thumpitty held his
breath and stared.

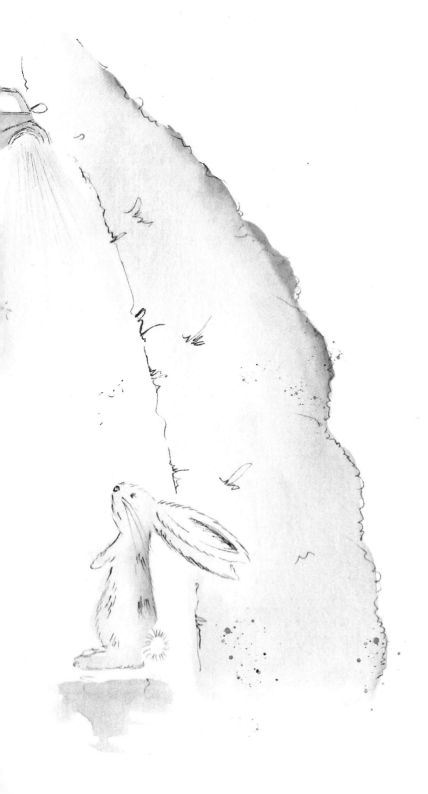

There was a mighty
crashing and with a
terrible roar,

two large
bright
eyes
appeared
at the
top of the
hill and
fixed
Thumpitty
with
a
stare.

for the first time in his life Thumpitty could not run.
He was so scared, his legs would not move.
The flashing glowing creature came nearer and nearer
and he felt its hot breath on him as it roared down,
when two huge paws grabbed his ears and pulled him
away.

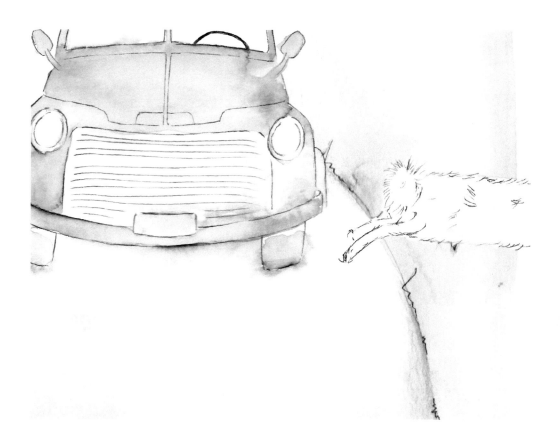

Thumpitty blinked his eyes and saw his "creature" was the farmers car, which was bumping its way down the hill, yellow lights winking as is bounced along.

He felt a warm face snuzzling against his and turned to see it was his mother who has saved him.

He told her how very, very sorry he was and she could see from his frightened eyes he had learned his lesson.

And now.....little
Thumpitty still loves to
run and race, but he
always plays where his
mother can see him
and he never, ever
goes through the hedge
to play in the road.

The End.